#4

# EINSTEIN ANDERSON
## SCIENCE DETECTIVE

# THE TIME MACHINE

## AND OTHER CASES

by Seymour Simon

illustrated by S. D. Schindler

**Morrow Junior Books**
**NEW YORK**

(Previously published as *Einstein Anderson Tells a Comet's Tale*)

*For all the "Einsteins"*
*I met while teaching*

Printed in the United States of America.

2   3   4   5   6   7   8   9   10

Library of Congress Cataloging-in-Publication Data
Simon, Seymour.
The time machine and other cases/by Seymour Simon;
illustrated by S. D. Schindler.—Rev. ed.
p. cm.—(Einstein Anderson, science detective)
Rev. ed. of: *Einstein Anderson tells a comet's tale*. 1981.
Summary: The sixth-grade science sleuth takes on ten more
puzzling cases, including one involving disappearing ice cream
and another, a speedy soapbox car.
ISBN 0-688-14441-1
[1. Science—Problems, exercises, etc.—Fiction.]   I. Schindler, S. D., ill.
II. Simon, Seymour. Einstein Anderson tells a comet's tale.   III. Title.
IV. Series: Simon, Seymour. Einstein Anderson, science detective.
PZ7.S60573Ti 1997   [Fic]—dc20   96-41765   CIP   AC

# CONTENTS

# 1
## The Case of the

# DANGEROUS COMET

"I wonder if you could meet me at my office today after school, Adam?" Mrs. Anderson asked her son at breakfast. "It's kind of important."

"I bet it has something to do with science, Einstein," said his younger brother, Dennis. "Whenever Mom wants you to meet her after school, she wants you to check on some science stuff for her."

"Sure, I'll be there," Einstein said. "Three-thirty be O.K.?"

Adam was the name the Andersons had

given to their first son. But most people called Adam Einstein, after the most famous scientist of the twentieth century. Adam had been interested in science even before he had started going to school. It was in kindergarten that his teacher and his friends had begun to call him by the nickname of Einstein. Adam was so good in using science to solve puzzles that even his teachers and his parents sometimes called him by his nickname.

"But it does have something to do with science, doesn't it, Mom?" Dennis persisted.

"Of course you're right, Dennis," Mrs. Anderson answered with affection. Mrs. Anderson was a writer and an editor on one of the town's newspapers, the Sparta *Tribune*. She often asked for Einstein's help in checking any science content in her stories.

"It's really very odd," Mrs. Anderson continued. "Someone named Dr. Edds wrote a letter to the paper about a book he just wrote. He says the book explains how the dinosaurs died out. And even more important, Dr. Edds claims that his theory forecasts the destruction of the human race."

"Wow," exclaimed Dennis. "It sounds exciting. Do you think there's anything to it, Einstein?"

"I can't tell till I hear what this Dr. Edds has to say," answered Einstein. "Meanwhile, it's time for us to catch the school bus. So like the dinosaur said to his brother, let's go pronto, Saurus."

When Einstein arrived at his mother's office that afternoon, Dr. Edds was already there. He was a large man, with a round reddish face. His heavy eyebrows waggled up and down as he talked.

"So your nickname is Einstein, young man," Dr. Edds said. "I suppose that's meant as a compliment, but I think Albert Einstein

made many mistakes, as I have pointed out in my book, *Comets in Collision.*"

"Is that right, sir," Einstein said politely. "I haven't seen your book, but I'd be interested in reading it. Have any scientists reviewed the evidence you present?"

Dr. Edds waved his hand airily. "Most scientists these days don't want to learn anything new. They are afraid my theories are correct and that all they have learned is worthless."

"What did they say about your book?" Einstein asked.

"In the future, people will call my book the

greatest scientific advance of the century," exclaimed Dr. Edds, his eyebrows moving up and down furiously. "And what some jealous reviewers say now doesn't bother me."

"Why don't you explain your theories to us, Dr. Edds," said Mrs. Anderson. "Then I will be able to write a column about them for my newspaper."

"With pleasure," said Dr. Edds. "I presume that you and your young son know what comets are?"

"Certainly," answered Mrs. Anderson.

"Comets?" Einstein said. "A comet is a collection of small rocks, dust, ice, and gases.

Comets revolve around the sun like planets. But their orbits are long and egg-shaped. At one end of its orbit a comet may come very close to the sun. But at the other end it may be out among the outer edges of our solar system."

"Very good, young man," said Dr. Edds. "But what about a comet's tail?"

"When a comet comes near to the sun, the gases begin to glow. The sun's rays push them away from the head, and they may form a tail hundreds of thousands of miles long."

"That's right," said Dr. Edds. "That's just what happens. And it is the basis of my theory. Comets rarely bother us. But once in a very long time a comet may come near the Earth. And even more rarely the comet may come so near to the Earth that we may pass through the comet's tail. When that happens, great disasters occur. In my book I hypothesize that the dinosaurs were killed off because of the poisonous gases in the tail of one of these comets."

Einstein pushed back his glasses and was about to say something when Mrs. Anderson asked, "Do you predict this is going to happen again?"

"My prediction is that the Earth will pass through the tail of a comet sometime in this century," Dr. Edds replied. "We must prepare ourselves for the tragedy. We need gas masks and shelters for ourselves and the animals we choose to save. All other life will be destroyed!"

"I see, sir," said Einstein. "I wonder if you would excuse me now. I have to do my homework."

"Would you excuse me for a minute also?" Mrs. Anderson said.

Outside her office Mrs. Anderson turned to Einstein and asked, "What do you think of Dr. Edds's theories? Should I get you a copy of his book to read? Is there any chance he may be right?"

"Don't bother," Einstein said. "Edds's tale is more full of hot air than a comet's."

*Can you solve the mystery:* How did Einstein know that Dr. Edds's theories were not worth worrying about?

"You mean scientists already know why the dinosaurs disappeared?" Mrs. Anderson asked.

"No one knows for sure," Einstein replied. "A recent theory is that a large asteroid may have hit the Earth sixty-five million years ago. Powdered rock from the Earth and the asteroid was thrown into the air and blocked out the sun for several years. Without sunlight, plants died. Dinosaurs starved to death. But that has nothing to do with Edds's theory about a comet's tail. You see, the Earth actually passed through the tail of Halley's comet in 1910, and absolutely nothing happened. A comet's tail is made of gases so thin they are almost a vacuum. In fact, a comet tail a million miles long could be stuffed into a suitcase."

"So Edds doesn't know what he's talking about."

"Right," Einstein said. "It's just too bad he doesn't have a brother or sister with him."

"Why is that?" Mrs. Anderson looked puzzled.

"Because two Edds are better than one!"

# 2
## The Case of the
# DISAPPEARING ICE CREAM

School had just let out for the day and Dennis was hungry as usual. "How about stopping in at Harper's drugstore for an ice-cream soda?" he asked Einstein.

"And who's going to pay?" asked his older brother. "I used up my allowance yesterday to buy some test tubes I needed. Besides, don't you owe me a dollar? Remember you borrowed it two weeks ago when you spent all your lunch money?"

"My treat," said Dennis airily. "Dad paid

me to help out at his office answering the phone yesterday afternoon. I'll pay back your loan with an ice-cream soda."

"Great," Einstein said. "It's a lucky thing Dad didn't get a mummy to answer the phone," he added.

"Why?" asked Dennis.

"A mummy can't answer a phone because he's all tied up."

"Sorry I asked," said Dennis.

When the boys arrived at Harper's drugstore, they noticed an ice-cream delivery truck parked outside. The driver of the truck was picking some ice-cream boxes off the street and loading them in the back of the truck. He was also muttering to himself and waving his hands.

"I wonder what's wrong," said Einstein.

"I don't know, but let's go in and get something to eat before you get involved," Dennis said.

The boys went into the store and sat down at the counter. In the mirror behind the counter Einstein could see Pat Burns in the back of the store, looking at a magazine. But

Einstein noticed he was holding the magazine upside down.

That's funny, Einstein thought. I wonder why Pat is pretending to read.

Pat Burns was in Einstein's sixth-grade class. He was the biggest boy in the grade and was always playing tricks on the other kids. His classmates called him Pat the Brat. But not to his face. He was too big and mean.

Just then the truck driver came into the store. He seemed very angry. "Did anyone see who opened the back of my truck and took out the ice cream?" he asked. "It's lucky I came back before it all melted."

"No, sir," said Dennis. "We just came into the store a minute ago."

"I didn't see anything either," said the counterman.

The driver looked around, and then saw Pat standing quietly by the magazines. "Did you see anything outside, kid?" he asked. "You must have been here for a while."

"Who, me?" said Pat. "I didn't do any-thing."

"I didn't accuse you," said the driver. "Say, wait a minute. Didn't I see you hanging around my truck when I left it to make a delivery?"

"Not me," said Pat. "I saw what happened

to your truck. I was reading this magazine when I heard a noise outside. I looked up just in time to see this other ice-cream truck reflected in the mirror behind the counter. The truck was parked right next to yours. The other truck driver must have taken out your ice cream."

"I didn't see any other truck," the driver said suspiciously. "Which company was it?"

"It was…er…Delicious Ice Cream Company," Pat said. "I read the name on the side of the truck."

"Never heard of it," said the driver.

"That's because Pat made up the whole story," Einstein whispered to Dennis.

"How do you know?" asked Dennis. "Pat could have seen a truck in the mirror."

*Can you solve the mystery:* How did Einstein know that Pat had made up the story about the other ice-cream truck?

"Say, Pat," said Einstein, "did you notice anything funny about the sign on the other ice-cream truck?"

"No," answered Pat. "I only saw the truck for a few seconds before it drove away. But I'm sure I read the sign on the side."

"And you read the sign in the mirror up here?" asked Einstein.

"That's right," said Pat angrily. "Why all the questions? That's what I saw!"

"Only that when you see things in a mirror, they are reversed. So the writing on the truck would be backward and not very easy to read quickly."

14

"Oh," said Pat. "Well, I gotta go now." He ran out the door before anyone could say anything.

The truck driver laughed. "I never saw anyone move so fast," he said. "I guess he had a guilty conscience."

"When Pat was in second grade," Einstein said, "he wanted to be a pirate. It's not everyone who gets to realize his ambitions."

# 3

## The Case of the

# LiGHTWEiGHT ROCKET

This time I've really had an idea that will make me famous," Stanley said over the phone. "Einstein," he continued, "I want you to come over to my house so I can tell you about it. If you help me with some of the minor details, I might even give you credit when I show my results to the world."

"You mean like the unbreakable glass you invented?" said Einstein. "You remember that invention. You convinced your parents to let you replace all the windows on the top floor of your house with your new glass. Everything went fine. Until it rained. Didn't the glass melt as soon as it got wet?"

"I wish you'd stop reminding me of that," Stanley replied. "Dad got so angry with me that he locked up my laboratory for a month."

Stanley Roberts was a junior in Sparta Senior High School. Even though Stanley was older than Einstein, they were good friends. Stanley was just as interested in science, but his experiments often had unexpected results. Stanley's "laboratory" was really an attic room that his parents let him use for his experiments.

"O.K., Stanley," Einstein said with a sigh. "Suppose I come over to your house after school tomorrow?"

"This invention is too exciting to wait. You've got to come over now. I'll see you in half an hour."

"But, Stanley," Einstein exclaimed, "I'm doing my homework now and I can't come over. Why don't you bring your invention over to my house?"

As usual, Stanley ignored him. After all,

17

Stanley was in high school while Einstein was only in sixth grade. "See you here in half an hour," he repeated, and hung up before Einstein could say anything.

Einstein put on a jacket and went downstairs. "I'm going over to visit Stanley," he called out.

"Don't be late for dinner," answered his mother. "And make sure you don't try out any of Stanley's experimental perfumes," she added.

"No chance of that, Mom," Einstein said. Stanley was always inventing new-smelling chemicals that smelled terrific—he said. But the last one he had tried out had smelled more like ripe bananas. Fruit flies had followed Stanley for a week before he could get rid of the odor.

"Before I go, I guess I might as well have a snack," Einstein said. In the kitchen, he opened the refrigerator and took out a bottle of milk, an apple, a few slices of bread, a jar of peanut butter, and a jar of jelly. He had just about finished when Mrs. Anderson came in.

"I hope you're not going to spoil your appetite," she said after looking at the remains of Einstein's "snack." "We're having cheeseburgers for dinner."

"Cheeseburgers," Einstein said thoughtfully. "Say, Mom, if the cheese comes after the meat, what comes after the cheese?"

"What?" said Mrs. Anderson.

"A mouse," Einstein said. "Gotta go now." He put the unused food back into the refrigerator and rinsed off the dishes. Then he waved and went out the door.

Along the way to Stanley's house Einstein examined some poison ivy leaves that were just beginning to turn bright red in the fall. He was careful not to touch the three-leaved plant. He also watched a squirrel gathering acorns and storing them in a hollow in a tree.

Einstein got to Stanley's house half an hour late. He rang the bell, and Stanley opened the door and motioned him to come inside. He tapped his watch and looked at Einstein. "I'll overlook your lateness," Stanley said. "Let's go up to the laboratory, and I'll show you the plans for my new invention."

When Einstein went into the attic, he saw that it was in its usual messy state. Pieces of what looked like rocket parts were scattered all over the floor. There was a metal tank labeled "Helium" standing by the lab table. The top of the table was covered with open books and with papers on which were all kinds of drawings.

"Wait till the National Aeronautics and Space Administration finds out what I've invented," Stanley said. "They'll be green with envy."

"If your invention is so great, you should have disconnected your doorbell," Einstein said.

"Why?" asked Stanley in a puzzled way.

"Because then you might win the No-bel prize," Einstein said.

"Ohh," Stanley groaned. "Why do you tell me those awful jokes? Do you want to hear about my invention or not?"

"Sure," said Einstein. "Haven't I given you the best ears of my life?"

Stanley paid no attention and began to show Einstein some drawings. "These are the plans of my new rocket," he said. "This big aluminum bubble in the middle of the rocket is going to be filled with helium."

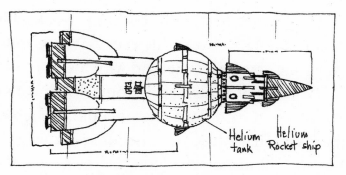

Helium tank   Helium Rocket ship

"Just a minute," Einstein said. "Helium can't be used for rocket fuel. It doesn't burn or support burning."

Stanley rubbed his hands together and laughed in his best imitation of a mad scientist. "The helium is not for fuel, my young friend," he said. "You know helium is a gas that is lighter than air. Well, I've designed a rocket that will be pumped full of helium. There will be so much helium that the rocket will weigh nothing. It will float. Then I can use a tiny engine and very little fuel to send the rocket to the moon or even to the planets."

"It *sounds* like a great idea," Einstein said. "Unfortunately, it can't work."

*Can you solve the mystery:* How does Einstein know that Stanley's rocket won't work?

21

Stanley pushed back his long black hair, which was falling over his eyes. "Where did I go wrong this time?" he said with a sigh.

"You really explained it yourself," Einstein said, "when you said that helium is lighter than air. That's true. But helium isn't weightless. It will make a balloon rise in air for the same reason that a piece of wood floats on water. But if you keep pumping helium into a rocket, it will just make the rocket heavier, in the same way that loading wood onto a ship just makes the ship heavier. And the heavier the rocket, the more fuel you will need."

"Then maybe we should just pump a little bit of helium into the rocket," Stanley said.

"That wouldn't work either," Einstein replied. "A little helium in a very light balloon will make it float because the balloon expands. The large balloon now weighs less than an equal amount of air. But pumping helium into a rocket doesn't make the rocket bigger, it just makes it heavier."

"I guess there's no point in my disconnecting the doorbell," Stanley said with a sad smile.

"Cheer up, old friend," said Einstein, pushing back his glasses. "Just think of how your doorbell is such a great help—to the knock need."

# 4

## The Case of the

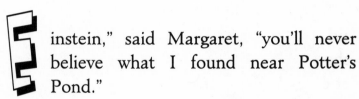
# MYSTERIOUS TRACKS

"**E**instein," said Margaret, "you'll never believe what I found near Potter's Pond."

"Why shouldn't I believe you, Margaret?" said Einstein. "Just because you're always trying to trick me into making a mistake in science?"

Margaret tried to hide a smile. "No, really," she said. "This is really weird. I can't understand what it is. Maybe you can explain it."

Margaret Michaels was Einstein's friend

and classmate. She was about as tall as Einstein and good at sports. She was also his rival in science. Einstein and Margaret were always doing science experiments together. They enjoyed talking to each other about important subjects such as atomic energy, spaceships, conservation—and who would get the highest grade on the next science test.

"You say you found something weird?" asked Einstein. "You mean weird like in UFOs or weird like in something natural that you don't understand?"

"It may be a little bit of both," Margaret said. "Suppose we walk up to the pond after school? It's only a mile away, and it doesn't get dark till five o'clock."

"It sounds interesting," admitted Einstein. "We should be able to walk there and still have time to catch the late bus."

The afternoon was cool and gray. As Einstein and Margaret walked along the bicycle path that led to the pond, the treetops bent and whispered in the wind. Once they saw a bird on a branch. Its black feathers made the bird difficult to see in the dim light.

It gave out a loud *caw* as they passed by.

"Look at the crow," said Einstein. "I hope it's not as cold as I am. Why don't you tell me about the weird thing you found? This is just the kind of day to hear about weird things."

"I found it yesterday," replied Margaret. "You remember that yesterday was nice and warm, not like today? I decided to ride my bike up to the pond. I spent some time looking for praying mantis egg cases in the bushes around the pond. I wandered over to a field, then I saw the strange tracks."

"Saw what?" Einstein asked.

"Well, the ground was muddy in the field, and I saw these large animal tracks in the mud."

"What kind of animal?"

"That's just it. I don't know. They were larger than any animal tracks I've ever seen. Even in books. And different too. It was scary. Wait till you see them."

Einstein shivered. "I can hardly wait," he said.

After a few more minutes of walking,

Margaret pointed to the left. "They're in this field over here," she said.

She walked into the field, and Einstein followed. "Here's where I found the tracks," she said.

Einstein bent down to look more closely. The tracks seemed to have been made by an animal, but they were larger than any Einstein had ever seen.

"It wasn't only the tracks that I saw yesterday," Margaret said. "I didn't realize how dark it had gotten. There was no moon, and I had no flashlight. I couldn't see anything. I was trying to find my bike when I heard this terrible growling noise in the bushes. I looked over, and I saw some animal eyes glowing in the dark. I turned and I ran. When I found my bike, I switched on the headlight and bicycled home as fast as I could."

Einstein looked at the tracks thoughtfully. Then he pushed his glasses back. "There's something peculiar about these tracks," he said. "In fact, they remind me of a story about a professor."

"What story is that?"

"It seems some students wanted to play a joke on their professor. So they glued together several different insect parts to make a single insect. Then they gave it to the professor to identify."

"Did it fool him?"

"Well, the professor examined the insect for a minute and then said that it was indeed a bug—in fact, it was a humbug."

"Why do the tracks remind you of that story?" asked Margaret, struggling not to laugh.

"Because that's what these tracks are. They're a humbug. Just like the rest of your story about the strange animal."

*Can you solve the mystery:* How did Einstein know that Margaret had made up the story about the strange animal tracks?

"But how do you know that, Einstein?" Margaret asked. "The tracks look real. And there's nothing wrong with my story, is there?"

"I wouldn't have been able to tell if you had just made the tracks and smudged them up a little bit. But your story is unbelievable."

"Why? What did I say that you don't believe?"

"Well, you probably wanted to make the story a little eerie, so you told me that the night was so dark that you couldn't see anything except an animal's eyes glowing. But that's impossible. An animal's eyes glow in the dark because they *reflect* light from some source. If there is no light to reflect, then they don't glow."

"I *knew* I should have made the story simpler and left out that part about the eyes," Margaret said. "Then I might have fooled you."

"That's true," Einstein agreed as they headed for the bus. "The eyes were a bad *eye, dear.*"

"So is that joke," groaned Margaret.

30

# 5

## The Case of the

# FASTEST KETCHUP iN THE CAFETERiA

The cafeteria at Sparta Middle School was always noisy at lunchtime. Today was no exception. There were fifth graders talking and standing on line at the food counter. There were sixth graders seated at tables, talking and eating their lunches. And there were even some from both grades running around yelling at everyone else.

Einstein and Margaret were sitting at a table along with their friends Sally and Mike. They were eating lunch—or rather they were poking at their food and mostly talking.

"This chicken is so tough," Einstein said, "it tastes like it hatched from a hard-boiled egg."

"Don't tell me you like the hot dogs any better," Margaret said. "Speak frankly, Einstein."

Einstein pushed back his glasses. "Well," he said, ignoring Margaret's pun, "I prefer the food that brave explorers eat."

"What kind of food is that?" Mike asked.

"Hero sandwiches, of course," Einstein said, and held his hands over his head as Mike threw a crumpled napkin at him.

"Uh-oh," Sally said. "Here come Pat and Herman. I hope they're not going to sit with us. Pat's always throwing food around. The last time he sat at a table with me, I ended the meal with more spaghetti in my hair than in my stomach. Maybe we can leave before they see us."

"It's too late to get up now," Margaret said. "Here they come."

"We're sitting at this table," Pat said. "So

shove over and make room for me and Herman."

"There's plenty of room for all of us," Einstein said. "Sit down and have some of my chicken. You'll love it."

"I got my own chicken," said Pat suspiciously. He sat down at the table and began to look around. "Any fifth graders around? I want to send one over to stand on line at the ice-cream counter."

"You may not be hungry after you finish the chicken," Einstein said in a low voice.

"Are you calling me chicken?" Pat asked. "Do you want to have a fight or something?"

"No, I didn't call you chicken, Pat. I was just talking about your food." Einstein was not afraid of Pat, but he tried to handle him by outthinking him rather than by outfighting him.

"O.K., Einstein," Pat said. "Somebody get me the ketchup. This chicken tastes like rubber."

Herman slid over a bottle of ketchup to Pat. "Here," he said.

Pat twisted off the cap on the bottle of ketchup and turned the bottle upside down over his plate. Nothing happened. Pat pounded the bottom of the bottle, and when still nothing happened, he held up the bottle to his eye. "This'll take forever," he said. "By the time I get some ketchup out of this bottle, lunch will be over. I think I'll bust the bottle and get some ketchup out that way."

"That'll get the ketchup out quick,"

Herman said. "You're real smart, Pat."

"Don't do that, Pat," Sally said. "You'll get ketchup and broken glass all over everything. And I don't want to wind up with ketchup all over my sweater. It took me long enough to wash out the spaghetti stains."

"You know any better way to do it?" Pat asked, holding the bottle of ketchup poised above the edge of the table.

"I do," Einstein said.

"Just because you know science doesn't mean you know how to pour ketchup," Pat said. "It takes strength to get ketchup out of a bottle. And I'm the one who's strong enough to do it."

"Science lets you do many things more easily," Einstein said, "including making ketchup pour quickly."

"If you can make this ketchup pour quickly without breaking the bottle, then I'll eat it all," Pat said.

"I hope you like ketchup," said Einstein.

*Can you solve the mystery:* How does Einstein plan to make the ketchup pour easily?

Einstein took the bottle of ketchup from Pat and replaced the cap. Then he shook the bottle vigorously up and down for a full minute. "Try it now," he said, giving the bottle back to Pat.

Pat took off the cap and started to hold the bottle up to his eye.

"Don't do that," Einstein said, "the ketchup will..."

The warning came too late. The ketchup poured down, covering Pat's face. "I'll get even with you for this!" Pat sputtered as he wiped ketchup out of his hair.

"I'm sorry that happened, Pat, but I tried to warn you," Einstein said. "Are you going to eat all that ketchup?" he asked innocently.

"Let's get out of here, Herman," Pat said, walking away without answering.

"How did you do that to the ketchup?" Margaret asked.

"Ketchup is an interesting kind of liquid," Einstein explained. "For one thing, there are solids mixed in with it. When the bottle has been standing for a while, the solids form a kind of supporting framework within the liquid. So the ketchup acts like a solid and doesn't flow."

"Then why did it pour out?" Mike asked.

"When I shook the bottle, the framework broke down. The ketchup acted like a liquid again and flowed out easily."

"Will the ketchup come out of that bottle easily from now on?" Sally asked.

"No," Einstein said. "The framework will form again if you let the ketchup stand quietly. Scientists even have a name for that kind of behavior. They called it thixotropy. Mayonnaise and honey act the same way."

"It's lucky Pat didn't get honey instead of ketchup in his hair." Sally laughed. "The bees would never leave him alone."

"Right," said Einstein. "And as the English say, he'd have to learn to beehive."

# 6

## The Case of the

# NOT-SO-DEAD FiSH

It was Election Day and the schools were closed. Dr. Anderson, Einstein's father, had voted early and then picked up Einstein. They were going to drive to the State Trout Hatchery near Big Lake State Park. Einstein was going because he was interested in seeing the hatchery and also because he liked to watch his father at work with animals. Dr. Anderson was a veterinarian.

"We're just going to make one stop before we get up to the hatchery," Dr. Anderson said. "Mr. Jackson wanted me to take a look at one of his milk cows."

"Doesn't Mr. Jackson also keep ducks?" Einstein asked.

"He has a few," Dr. Anderson said. "Why do you ask?"

"Well, if Mr. Jackson crosses one of his cows with one of his ducks, he'll have milk and quackers."

"Adam," said Dr. Anderson, "that's a terrible joke. Next you'll be telling me that the reason cows wear bells is because their horns don't work."

Einstein started to laugh. "No," he said. "I was going to ask you what they call cows that live in the Arctic."

"What?" Dr. Anderson asked cautiously.

"Eskimoos," said Einstein.

"I give up," said Dr. Anderson. "Please, no more puns."

"Sure, Dad," Einstein said. "Why are you going up to the trout hatchery?"

"I got a call yesterday from Dr. Susan Stein, the biologist in charge of the hatchery. She invited me up to see them stripping the eggs from the trout. I thought you'd be interested, so I decided to take you up with me."

"Thanks, Dad," Einstein said. "I've been up at the hatchery before, but I've never seen them remove the eggs. How do they do it?"

"One of the ponds is just stocked with fish for egg production. The largest females are kept there; they'll produce the most eggs. Around this time of year the females are taken out and held over a water-filled pan. Their bodies are gently squeezed, and eggs come out into the pan. The same females are stripped of eggs for several years in succession."

"That doesn't harm the fish, does it?" Einstein asked.

"Not at all," Dr. Anderson said. He turned his car off the main road. "There's Mr. Jackson's farm," he said. "This visit shouldn't take long. We'll be up at the hatchery before lunch."

Dr. Anderson was as good as his word. He and his son arrived at the hatchery at eleven o'clock. Dr. Stein came up to them as they parked the car. "How are you, David?" she said, shaking hands with Dr. Anderson.

"Fine, and you, Susan? I'd like you to meet my son, Adam."

"Glad to meet you, Dr. Stein," Einstein said. "I can't wait to see the hatchery again," he added.

"Come on then," said Dr. Stein. "Let me show you what we're doing. We're stripping eggs now."

Dr. Stein led them to a pool where the trout were being removed and the eggs stripped into pans. "After the eggs are stripped," she said, "they are fertilized with milt stripped from the reproductive glands of the males. Then we take the fertilized eggs into a building so that they can hatch under controlled conditions. The eggs are small and jellylike. We keep the eggs in flowing water at fifty degrees Fahrenheit. Most of them hatch in about five weeks."

"The young are called fry, aren't they?" Einstein said.

"That's right," said Dr. Stein. "When the fry get large enough, they are placed in ponds. Each size fry has its own pond, because the different sizes need different amounts of food. The trout are kept for a year and a half. Then they are placed in streams during the spring."

"How is everything going this year at the hatchery?" asked Dr. Anderson.

"Not too well," Dr. Stein admitted. "We don't have enough money to hire a watchman, and someone has been taking trout out of our breeding pond. In fact, we've lost almost a hundred large females in the last two months."

"That's too bad," Dr. Anderson said. "Let me take a look at your records. Maybe I can raise some private funds to help you restock. Why don't you look around the hatchery, Einstein, while Dr. Stein and I talk in her office?"

"O.K.," Einstein said. "But please don't take too long. I'm getting hungry."

Einstein wandered around the hatchery. He saw that there were at least twenty ponds spread out over the grounds. Some were long and narrow, while others were round. Einstein stopped to watch two men kneeling by one of the ponds that held the large female trout used in breeding. The men were taking fish from the pond and putting them in a basket.

Einstein walked over and asked, "What are you doing? Are you taking those fish in to be stripped?"

The men turned to look at Einstein and closed the basket quickly. "We work at the hatchery. These fish are dead," one said. "We're taking them out of the pond so they won't rot."

"That's funny," said Einstein. "They didn't look dead to me."

"Sure they're dead," said the man. "You can tell they're dead when their eyes close."

"I see," said Einstein. He turned and walked toward the office. When he got out of sight, he started to run as fast as he could.

Those men don't work here, he said to himself. They must be the ones who are taking the trout.

*Can you solve the mystery:* How does Einstein know the men are not workers at the hatchery?

Einstein knocked on the door to Dr. Stein's office, then ran inside. "I just saw some men taking trout out of one of your breeding pools," he said to Dr. Stein. "They said they were working here at the hatchery, but they made an awful mistake about fish when I asked them a question."

"They must be the ones stealing our trout," said Dr. Stein. "I'll call the state police right away. There's only one way out of the hatchery, and the police can block it off." Dr. Stein went over to the phone and began to dial.

"How did you know the men weren't working here?" Dr. Anderson asked his son.

"One of the men said he knew the fish he was taking were dead because their eyes were closed. But even a dead fish can't close its eyes. Fish don't have eyelids."

"That wasn't very smart of him," Dr. Anderson said.

"No," said Einstein. "He must have been a fugitive from a brain gang."

# 7

## The Case of the

## STRANGE CLUES

argaret was having a birthday party at her house. Einstein and most of her other classmates were there. The theme of the party was science fun. Margaret had made all kinds of special treats, such as meteor burgers (made with hot sauce), nuclear popcorn (it popped with a bang), and cookies in the shape of stars.

They also played games, such as guessing people's weight—on Mars, Jupiter, and the moon. During science-fiction charades Margaret had to act out the movie title

*Invasion of the Body Snatchers.* Nobody on her team guessed what she was doing. Einstein didn't help by making believe that he thought Margaret was acting out *Bride of Frankenstein.*

After everyone had a chance at charades (Pat did *King Kong,* and his team guessed immediately), Margaret got up to speak.

"Now it's time for the main event," she said. "I've made up a special treasure hunt. Each person is going to get a mysterious rhyme. The rhymes will have clues to other clues that are hidden around the house. And in keeping with the theme of my party, the clues are all science clues."

"That's not fair," objected Pat. "Einstein will win easy. He knows more science than anybody else."

"We'll see about that," Margaret said. "I've made up special clues for Einstein. They're a little harder than anyone else's clues. In fact, they're a great deal harder."

"Wait a minute, Margaret," Einstein said. "That's not fair. Maybe you can just make them a little harder."

"Nothing doing, Einstein," Margaret said.

"If I can make up the clue, you should be able to solve them—at least if you know as much science as you say you do. Are you going to accept?"

Einstein nodded. He just couldn't turn down a challenge from Margaret.

"O.K. then. Is everybody ready? Here's a copy of treasure rhymes for each one of you. And here's your special rhyme, Einstein. You can start searching as soon as you want to."

In a few seconds the boys and girls were off on the chase. Einstein looked down at his rhyme. It didn't even make sense. Here is what it said:

> The first clue has no words in sight.
> For number two you'll need some light.
> The third one's hidden in between.
> To find the treasure, use your bean.

Then there was a little note that said: "Einstein, you'll find the first clue in the room that contains green moon material."

Einstein pushed back his glasses. I'll begin with the note about the room, he thought to himself. The moon isn't green.... Wait a minute. Of course! There was an old fable that said the moon was made of green cheese. And cheese would be in the kitchen.

"So long, Margaret," Einstein said. "I have to go look at some cheese. I guess I'll look Kraftily."

Einstein hurried into the kitchen. On the counter next to the toaster was a hunk of cheese and a sheet of paper. Einstein picked up the paper. It was blank.

"The first clue has no words in sight," he said thoughtfully. "But there must be something on the paper." Einstein looked at the cheese, then at the toaster. That must be it, he thought.

After a minute of working on the paper, he found another message. The clue read: "You'll find the second clue in the room where 'living creatures dance in a drop of rainwater.'"

Well, thought Einstein, that sounded like Van Leeuwenhoek, the first one to really use a microscope, way back in 1675, when he observed the tiny things around him. The little "creatures" were tiny water animals, such as protozoa. And a microscope would be in Margaret's room, which she also used as a lab.

Einstein ran up the stairs to Margaret's room. He switched on the light and looked around. Sure enough, there was the microscope on the table. But there was no paper next to it. Where could the clue be? he wondered.

The rhyme said, "For number two you'll need some light." But there was light in the room. Could the microscope have anything to do with the clue? That's it, Einstein decided.

In a few seconds Einstein was reading the second clue. It said: "You'll find the third clue no easy medicine to take."

Well, the next room is easy, Einstein thought. Medicine must be in the cabinet in the bathroom.

Einstein went into the bathroom next to Margaret's bedroom. There was a sheet of paper propped up between a bottle of castor oil and a bottle of cod-liver oil. Margaret was right about no easy medicine, Einstein thought.

Einstein examined the paper. It seemed to be two sheets pasted together. The rhyme said, "The third one's hidden in between." He held up the sheets to a bright light. He could make out some words, but they were impossible to read.

I can't rip the paper apart, Einstein thought. That might destroy the clue. He looked at the castor oil and the cod-liver oil. That was the medicine, all right, he decided.

In less than a minute Einstein was downstairs in the room with Margaret. "O.K, Margaret," he said, "here's the saying you wrote on the third clue: 'Why was Eve the first scientist?' And the answer is that she knew all about the Adam."

Margaret laughed. "You win," she said. "Now tell me how you got to the clues."

*Can you solve the mysteries:* 1. How did Einstein make the first clue visible? 2. Where was the second clue hidden? 3. How was Einstein able to read the clue between the sheets of paper?

"Well," Einstein said, "the green moon material must have been cheese, so that meant the kitchen. Then I saw the blank piece of paper. The words weren't in sight, so you must have written them in some kind of invisible ink such as vinegar or lemon juice. The writing will become visible if it's heated, because the lemon juice combines with oxygen and changes color. So I used the toaster, which you left near the paper."

"I figured you'd get that clue," Margaret said. "What about the second clue?"

"Because you used the Leeuwenhoek quote, I looked in the room where you keep your microscope. Microscopes need a light either reflected by a mirror or a special lamp to work well, so that was your clue about needing light. I looked at the microscope and found your message on a slide that you had prepared. That led me to the medicine cabinet."

"But how did you read the final message? I had pasted it between two sheets of paper."

"That was the most difficult to figure out. But then I realized that the castor oil and the cod-liver oil are not just medicines, they are also *oils*. I spilled a little oil on the sheet of paper. The paper became translucent—light goes through it much more easily. Then I could read your final puzzle without any trouble."

"Next time I'll make the clues more difficult," Margaret said with a sigh.

"Don't be sad," said Einstein, "because I'm going to treat you like a blue monster."

"How do you treat a blue monster?" Margaret asked.

"You cheer her up," said Einstein.

# 8

## The Case of the

# TiME MACHiNE

**E**instein," Stanley said, "you'll never believe the science photographs I just received in the mail."

"I probably won't," said Einstein. "I hope they're not photos of giant ants or green monsters."

"I wish you'd forget about those mistakes I made," Stanley said. "They could have happened to anyone. How was I to know that green-monster advertisement was a fake?"

"True," Einstein said. "After all, there

really is only one thing that's green and dangerous."

"What's that?" asked Stanley, suddenly becoming very interested.

"A thundering herd of pickles," replied Einstein with a smile.

"That joke is silly even for you," Stanley said. "Do you want to see the photographs or not?"

"Sure," said Einstein. "Show me the photographs in a flash."

Stanley groaned. "Please stop the jokes. This is serious. In one of the magazines I was reading I found an advertisement for the complete plans for a time machine."

"A time machine?" Einstein was startled. "You don't mean to tell me you paid money for that kind of nonsense! A time machine is impossible!"

"Why do you say that?" asked Stanley.

"Suppose there was a time machine," Einstein said. "And suppose someone used it to go back in time and shoot the man who invented the time machine before he invented it. So the time machine never got invented, so the man never went back in time, so the inventor was never shot. You can see that the whole thing becomes logically impossible."

"But that's just it," Stanley said triumphantly. "This time machine doesn't carry people. It only carries a camera. The camera takes a picture of the past or the future and then returns to the present."

"I still don't believe it."

"Well, neither did I," Stanley admitted. "So I wrote to the people in the advertisement and asked for proof. They sent me these pictures of the past and of the future. And they look real to me." Stanley held out two photographs to Einstein.

Einstein examined them curiously. One of the photographs was of a modern-looking city. It showed what appeared to be glass or plastic domes covering large parklike areas. Outside the domes was a desolate rocky landscape. The caption under the photograph read, "Life domes on the moon in A.D. 2180."

The other photograph showed two people in togalike robes, sitting at a table and eating from a large clay dish. Behind one of them was a clock with a single hand pointing to the Roman numeral XII. On the wall was a painting of a chariot being pulled by horses. The man in the chariot was wearing armor and a helmet that looked like those of a Roman soldier. The caption under the photograph read, "Citizens of Rome eating lunch in their home in the year A.D. 22."

Einstein pushed back his glasses thoughtfully. "It's difficult to tell anything from these photographs," he said. "But there is one serious mistake that proves that the photos are phony."

*Can you solve the mystery:* What is the mistake that convinced Einstein that the photos were not genuine?

Stanley shook his head sadly. "What's the mistake?" he asked.

"It's in the photograph of Roman times," Einstein replied. "There's something in that photo that couldn't possibly exist in Roman times."

"It all looks old to me," said Stanley.

"Not old enough," Einstein said. "It's true that the clock on the wall in the photo has Roman numerals and a single hand, but it's more than a thousand years too early. The first mechanical clocks were not invented till the thirteenth century. The Romans used sundials to tell time, not clocks."

"Can you imagine those crooks trying to fool me!" Stanley exclaimed.

"You can't fool anyone with a clock on the wall," Einstein said.

"Why not?" Stanley asked, bracing himself for Einstein's answer.

"Because time will tell."

# 9

## The Case of the

# GRIZZLY MISTAKE

Y ou'll just have to forget about science for the next hour, Einstein," Ms. Warren, Einstein's social studies teacher, said. "We're learning about the history of the development of Alaska, and there is no science involved in this particular discussion. So please pay attention and put that science book away."

"Yes, Ms. Warren," Einstein replied. "But everything's connected with science in some way."

"Why don't you tell us if you find anything scientific in Alaska's history," Ms. Warren said impatiently. "But until then would you please do what the rest of the class is doing."

"Yeah, Einstein, just be quiet," said Pat. "How can I concentrate on all this history stuff if you keep talking about science?"

"Oh, are you concentrating, Pat?" Margaret said sweetly. "I thought I smelled wood burning."

The class groaned. Ms. Warren rang a bell on her desk. "Will everyone please quiet down," she said. "We've had enough of this nonsense. Let's go back to work. I'm going to read from several journals kept in the Klondike about the time of the gold rush. You'll see how difficult times were back in those frontier days."

Ms. Warren reached for a book from a pile on top of her desk. She opened it to a place mark. "This book is by a man nicknamed Grizzly Sam. It tells the story of one of the gold discoveries that took place in Alaska in 1896."

Ms. Warren began to read.

"When I woke up on the morning of January thirtieth, the temperature was twenty degrees below zero. It was a clear day, but the wind was blowing something fierce. After a hurried breakfast I started out for the diggings. Before I got halfway there, I saw a grizzly. It must have been looking for food, but when it spotted me, it started coming.

"I ran across a frozen pond near my cabin, but the ice must have been thin in spots, and I fell through. Luckily, the water wasn't deep, but I did get soaked. I ran as fast as I could back to the cabin, which was about a mile away.

"The grizzly stopped chasing me for some reason or other, but I was so cold that I kept on running. When I got back to the cabin, my soaking clothes made a big puddle on the floor. I got out of them and got dressed in some dry clothes. This time I was going to be ready for any grizzlies. I took my rifle along with me."

"Excuse me, Ms. Warren," Einstein said, raising his hand.

"What is it now, Einstein?" asked Ms. Warren.

"I'm sorry to interrupt the story, but I thought you'd like to know that it doesn't make sense, scientifically."

"Is that so?" said Ms. Warren. "How can you be so sure? You don't know firsthand what conditions were like in Alaska at that time. And what does science have to do with it, anyway?"

"Science tells me that one part of Grizzly Sam's story is just not possible. And if that one part is just a made-up story, I wonder if anything in his journal can be trusted."

*Can you solve the mystery:* What part of Grizzly Sam's story is not scientifically possible?

65

"You mean that you don't believe the part about being chased by a grizzly?" Ms. Warren asked. "But many prospectors have recounted stories of adventures with aggressive grizzly bears."

"There's nothing unscientific about that," Einstein said. "A grizzly might very well chase a person. It's another part of the story that I don't believe. Grizzly Sam wrote that the temperature was twenty degrees below zero and that a strong wind was blowing. It's hardly likely that anyone would try to work a mine under those conditions."

"Well, maybe he just wanted to look at it," said Pat. "You can't call him a liar just because *you* wouldn't go out in the cold."

"I think Pat is right about that," Ms. Warren said. "How can you be sure Sam wouldn't have gone out?"

"Because the rest of his story is impossible. Sam said that he fell through the ice of a pond and got soaked. Then he ran back to his cabin, which was a mile away. When he got to the cabin, he said, his clothes were soaking and they made a puddle on the floor."

"Well, if your clothes are wet, they drip," Pat said.

"Not if you run through air at twenty degrees below zero," said Einstein. "Sam's clothes would have frozen. They wouldn't be soggy, and they couldn't drip on the floor."

Ms. Warren thought for a moment. "I think you're right, Einstein," she said. "If Grizzly Sam made up one part of his story, he may have made up other details as well."

"I knew you couldn't trust what Sam wrote," said Einstein. "After all, didn't you tell us he slept in a *bunk* bed?"

# 10
## The Case of the
# SPEEDY
# SOAPBOX CAR

Thanksgiving was coming up, and the seventh graders were determined to beat the sixth graders in a contest before the holiday, regardless of what Einstein would do.

During lunch break a group of seventh graders came up to Einstein, Margaret, Sally, and Mike.

"The seventh grade challenges the kids in the sixth grade to a soapbox race," said Tom, one of the seventh graders. "Our class will make one soapbox racer and your class will make one."

"Will there be any rules?" Margaret asked him cautiously.

"Yeah," said Tom. "The first soapbox to reach the bottom wins. Ha, ha."

"Very funny," Margaret said. "Almost as funny as our beating you will be."

"The only way you can beat us is if we let Einstein talk us into some crazy rules."

"Well, you're older and bigger than we are," Einstein said. "So it's only fair that we're allowed to use our brains to make the contest fairer."

"Are you trying to say you're smarter than us?"

"Who, me?" Einstein said innocently. "I think the seventh grade has a rare intelligence...very rare."

"We'll see about that," answered Tom. "Let's make the contest really interesting. The losers have to serve the winners in the cafeteria for two weeks."

"Why don't we make it for a month?" Margaret said.

"You're on," said the seventh grader. "Now let's set the rules for the race. We want to make sure that Einstein doesn't come up with something scientific to make the sixth grade win."

In a short time the rules for the race were set. The soapbox racers were to be made only of scrap wood and old baby carriage wheels. The total weight had to be thirty pounds or less. The soapboxes were to have one ten-foot push on the top of the hill by the driver. The rest of the way they had to coast down the hill on their own.

The contest was set for the Wednesday afternoon just before Thanksgiving. The race would take place on the unused dirt road that went straight down Turner's Hill for just about half a mile.

Einstein was glum when the seventh graders left. "I don't think you should have made the bet for a month, Margaret," he said. "We might easily lose."

"There must be some way that we can use science to help us," said Margaret. "Let's just make a faster soapbox racer."

"That's easier said than done," Einstein said. "The weight has to be the same and the wheels have to be old baby carriage wheels. The push on the top of the hill is the same. I'm sure that the seventh grade will try to streamline the racer to cut down on wind drag just as we will. What else can we do?"

"You mean we might lose?" Sally asked. "That would be awful! Who wants to serve the seventh graders for a month!"

"Let me think," Einstein said. He pushed back his glasses. "There *is* one thing that might work," he said after a minute.

The weather was beautiful the afternoon of the race. The seventh graders wheeled out their soapbox racer. It was sleek and low to the ground. It had been painted a bright blue. The sixth-grade racer looked much the same. The only difference was that it was much higher off the ground and it was painted a bright red.

*Can you solve the mystery:* How had Einstein planned to win the soapbox derby?

In a few minutes the soapboxes were at the starting line. Einstein was the driver of the sixth-grade soapbox, while Tom, the strongest seventh grader, was going to drive their racer. When the starting signal was given, both drivers pushed their boxes for ten feet, then leaped aboard.

The seventh-grade racer had a slight lead at the start. The distance between the racers stayed about the same at the smooth top of the hill. But when the racers got to the bumpy middle part of the hill, Einstein's soapbox began to catch up. Soon it was in the lead and lengthening the distance. By the end of the race Einstein's soapbox was more than twenty feet in front.

The sixth graders were cheering and yelling. The seventh graders were quiet and just looked disgusted. "That Einstein ought to be banned from contests," one seventh grader said. "He always comes up with something."

Afterward Einstein explained to his friends why the sixth-grade soapbox had won. "It's because of the size of the wheels," he said. "Their racer looks nicer because it's built so low to the ground. But their baby carriage wheels have to be small to get the racer low. Our racer doesn't look as good, because the wheels are the biggest ones we could find."

"But what difference does that make?" Mike asked. "The wheels have to cover the same distance, don't they?"

"That's true," Einstein said. "But a smaller wheel has to turn many more times than a larger wheel to cover the same distance. That means there is much more friction in the smaller wheel, and that slows it down more."

"But why were you able to go so much faster over the bumpy part of the hill?" Margaret asked.

"Because the force needed to make a small wheel go over rocks and bumps is much greater than the force needed for a large wheel. Since the force of gravity helped both racers the same amount, the sixth-grade racer could go much faster. That's why the old covered wagons had such large wheels. They were so much easier to push over rocks than wagons with smaller wheels."

"The sixth grade knew you wouldn't let us down," Sally said.

"Well, scientists know how to always win a race," Einstein said.

"Really?" Margaret said. "How can anyone always win?"

"By always coming in first," said Einstein.